The Island and the Bear

Louise Greig & Vanya Nastanlieva

Picture Kelpies

Anything can happen anywhere.
Anywhere was an island.
Anything was a bear.

Yes, a bear!
Just suddenly there, filling the air with bear.
He was as brown as the earth and as big as a tree
and when he shook, gulls rose from the sea!

And when he roamed, lambs quivered in fear!
Please bear, they bleated, *go home!*
Here was a bear where a bear should not be.
The islanders scattered like stones.

The sea came in and the salt came in
but the sea did not taste right.
There was no sweet morsel in sight.

This island is good, but where is the food?
roared the bear from the loftiest height.

But the sound of his voice made the sea run out
and the wind blow backwards with fright!

I will ask the people and the sheep,
thought the bear.
They will know what a bear can eat!

Hello! roared the bear from the shore.
Some people hid. Some people fled.
"This island is not meant for bears," they said.

They boarded their doors with tables and chairs
and trembled like reeds in the snow.
"Please bear," they pleaded, "please go."

The island held its breath.
What would the bear do next?

When the bear loped off,
they learned the truth: he was lost.
Onto the island two hearts stepped.
"We are searching for our bear," they wept.

"Let us help you," some islanders said.
"With the small of our island and the
big of your bear,
he's bound to appear again somewhere."

They looked north and south and east and west,
and the hills were there and the gulls were there
and the sheep were there,
but – no sign of a bear.

The bear tilted his ears to the drum
of the wind and the surge of the sea.
His fur ruffled in the breeze.

He began to dance
in the blink of the sun.
The bear and the island were one!

But the bear was getting hungry.

Oh look, how kind, he suddenly sang,
someone has left apples for me.

Now it's time for a swim, thought the bear,
as into the blue loch he crashed
and happily dived and splashed.
Brown bear, brown salmon, brown trout!
The bear did not want to come out!

But the tiny fish fled, too scared to swim.
Though he would not harm a living thing.
No never.
Not ever.
Not ever.

Now, the hungry bear thought, *what's for lunch?*
A sandwich. Delicious! Munch, crunch.

A small girl saw. The wind blew.
She heard the bear say, *Thank you.*
And then she knew.

This bear from out of the blue was good!
And then, once again, he was gone.

Quietly, they came forward and left more food.
"Forgive us," they cried. "We misunderstood."

But the girl from the wild island croft
knew where the lonely bear was.
Gently, she reached out her hand
and murmured, "I understand."

Her eyes held the silver light of the sea.
"Come bear," she whispered. "Come with me.
Someone is missing you."
And the bear as big as a tree
felt suddenly weary.
He missed someone too.

And so it was that a child with the wind in her hair,
brought back together two hearts and a bear.

The islanders watched in fading light
as the bear grew smaller and smaller into the night.

Suddenly the island felt huge with *goodbye*.

Until something appeared in the sky.

Anything can happen anywhere.
Anywhere was an island.
Anything was a bear.

Goodnight all bears,
wherever you are sleeping.